# GIRAFFE
## IS GRUMPY

To Mud Masters:
Wyatt, Aloha, and JoJo
— H.L.

ISBN 978-1-338-84931-8
10 9 8 7 6 5 4 3 2 1     23 24 25 26 27
Printed in the U.S.A.     40
This edition first printing, October 2023

# GIRAFFE
## IS GRUMPY

by Hilary Leung

Scholastic Inc.

# Giraffe is grumpy.
# His friends want to cheer him up...

...but will Giraffe laugh?

# Will Giraffe laugh with Bear?

No.

# Will Giraffe laugh with Crocodile?

Oh, no.

# Will Giraffe laugh with Sheep?

Ouch! No.

# Will Giraffe laugh with Frog?

# Nope.

# Will Giraffe laugh with Ladybug?

Achoo!

NOOOOOOOOOOOOOOO...

Uh-oh.
Will Giraffe cheer up
his friends?

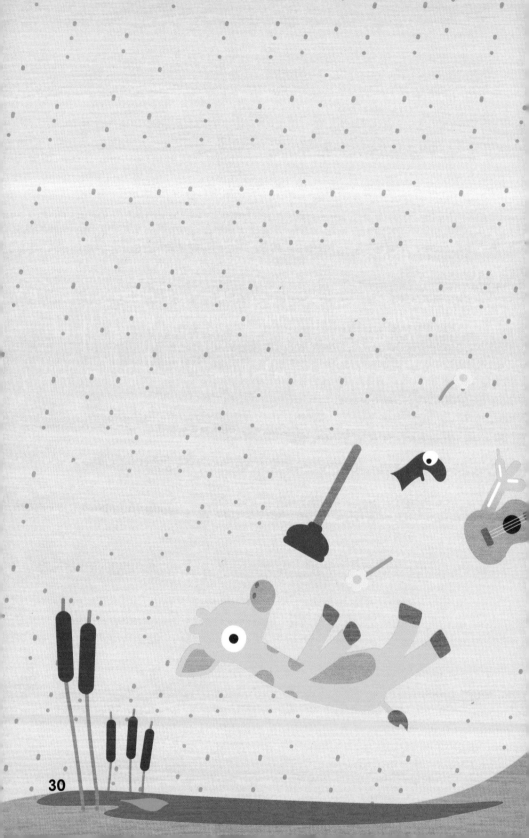

# Haha, yes!

# How do you cheer up your friends?